From Tolerable to Lovely

A TEATIME TALES
NOVELETTE

LEENIE BROWN

Leenie B Books
Halifax

Cover design by Leenie B Books. Images sourced from Deposit Photos and Period Images.

ISBN: 978-1-989410-68-4 (ebook); 978-1-990607-44-8 (paperback); 978-1-990607-45-5 (large print)

www.leeniebbooks.com

www.leeniebrown.com

Chapter 1

FITZWILLIAM DARCY WISHED TO rub his temples or pinch the bridge of his nose – anything to stop the throbbing behind his eyes that accompanied the incessant babbling of his overly gregarious friend. He wanted to relieve his discomfort, but he could not. He would not display such flagrant disdain for his friend's exuberance. At least, he would not do so here. Had they been in private, he would have told his friend in rather ungentlemanly terms to cease speaking. But, they were not in private – far from it!

The completion of a set of dances brought with it a small bit of relief as the music stopped and the room was left with just the cacophony of voices to fill its length, breadth, and height. Thankfully, most who were standing along the edges of the room adjusted the volume of their voices accordingly. However, there were a few who did not. There were always a few at these sorts of events who either cared not that their voice carried from one end of the dance floor to the other, or they had imbibed a trifle too freely of the beverages which were on offer.

A crowded assembly room was not a place where Darcy liked to spend much time. He was only in this one because he could not convince his friend to leave him at Netherfield.

Darcy drew a silent fortifying breath. Bingley's attention, which had been momentarily distracted by some new acquaintance with a daughter in need of a husband who possessed a sizeable fortune, as Bingley did, was once again turned toward Darcy. If only he could speak plainly to Bingley. But he could not. His current surroundings demanded that he attempt to use subtlety to inform his friend that no amount of constant nattering was going to persuade him to dance.

And that was the problem. Bingley was almost entirely incapable of recognizing subtlety, and the more enamored he was with his circumstances and the more excited he was about whatever possibility he was presenting, the less likely he was to hear subtlety. Charles Bingley was not stupid. Far from it! However, he was easily distractible when presented with lively entertainment and pretty ladies.

Darcy tried to focus on the stream of praise for their current surroundings coming from his friend. How could Bingley find such environs to be worthy of notice, let alone praise? Darcy had never, in the entirety of his life, enjoyed being in a room, filled to overflowing, with people, nor had he ever discovered the delight which some found in dancing.

To him, a room crowded with people – the majority of whom were strangers – all gawking at him, whispering about him, and measuring him with their chosen standard, be it clothing, disposition, looks, or wealth, had always been akin to tolerable torture. However, after recent events in his life, the whispers had grown louder, the looks had become more calculated, and Darcy had begun to feel less and less like a horse, being appraised by a potential new owner at Tattersalls, and more and more like a fish at the fishmongers, being haggled over by the cook who would be serving him on a platter at some elegant dinner.

Had Bingley not noticed the way the mothers had pushed their daughters forward into his path? Had he not noticed the cunning look of the huntress as she prepared to ensnare her prey? Pleasant company? Hardly. The room was too small, too lacking in air, and too abundant in fragrance – not all of which were pleasing to the nose.

"Darcy, you simply must dance."

Darcy shook his head slightly and gave his friend a hard glare. He had already done his duty in dancing with both of Bingley's sisters, who were just as shrewd as any of the mothers in attendance, though, perhaps, Miss Bingley and Mrs. Hurst were a bit more wily having practiced their techniques in the venues of the ton. What more could Bingley want?

"Come now. You must dance. You cannot just stand about all night."

Dance? Had Bingley suggested dancing – again? Obviously, Bingley, in his exuberance, was unwilling or unable to comprehend the stare that Darcy had given him. A more direct approach seemed necessary.

"As you know, I do not like dancing, and I shall not be moved to do so."

Did his friend have any idea how trying, how uncomfortable, how utterly unbearable it was to be introduced to new people, to fumble for words, and to act the part of the master of Pemberley as people expected? Had he not told Bingley of his struggles with conversation?

The throbbing behind Darcy's eyes grew with his frustration. He sighed. Bingley was now extolling the beauty of the ladies present. Darcy knew that his friend had found one lady to be of particular interest. Bingley always found one to capture his interest for the length of an evening. However, none of them kept his attention for longer than a week or two if she was fortunate enough not to be replaced at the beginning of a new day.

The beauty whom Bingley had settled upon at this ball was a handsome blonde who smiled very willingly at one and all. She was far too agreeable for Darcy's liking, but it would not do to insult his friend's preference.

"You are dancing with the only handsome girl in the room." Darcy hoped that such a mention would turn the conversation to Bingley's opinion of his dancing partner and, with any luck, send him off in search of her. For a moment, it seemed to work.

"Miss Bennet is lovely is she not? I dare say I have never met another who compares to her."

"She is a beauty."

"As are her sisters. In fact, there is one of her sisters sitting down just behind you, who is very pretty, and I dare say very agreeable. I shall ask Miss Bennet to introduce you." Bingley made to step away.

Darcy's arm shot out to stay his friend. Panic coursed through him. Was Bingley actually going to arrange the introduction without waiting for Darcy's consent?

"What do you mean? There is a pretty sister where?"

"Just there, behind you."

Darcy looked to see of whom his friend was speaking.

"The one who is talking to the lady next to her," Bingley whispered. "In the green dress."

The dress, which the lady, whom Bingley had indicated, wore was not so fashionable as some, but the colour did compliment her creamy complexion and brown hair with its tinges of copper. She was a rather pretty lady who seemed out of place sitting amongst the wallflowers. Why would someone so lovely as she be sitting down rather than dancing? She must have some defect. He stared at her, as he wondered what would prevent her from not having a partner for every dance – until she looked up. Soft brown eyes caught his. Startled, he looked away.

She was not just pretty. She was captivating. However, it would not do for Bingley to know that Darcy found Miss Bennet's sister to be attractive. Armed with such information, Bingley would become as unrelenting as Darcy's best hunting dog, chasing and manoeuvring until his prey – in this case, Darcy – was cornered. He must be as direct and as ruthless as possible to stop the attack before it could be launched. Such a tactic made him uneasy, but Darcy knew that a bit of prevarication was necessary. Where was the harm in it? It was Bingley to whom he was speaking. Bingley would tease him about it later, but he would not share what Darcy said with anyone.

In a low, indifferent tone, Darcy said, "She is tolerable, but not handsome enough –"

His words were interrupted when Bingley grabbed him by the arm and spun both of them out of the way of a gentleman – a Mr. Dalton if Darcy remembered correctly – who was attempting to steady his partner and save her from the complete humiliation of a fall. Darcy watched as the young lady regained her footing and continued in the dance. He shook his head, and an amused smile tugged at his lips. It was the first time he had felt any amusement in months.

"I do believe that young lady's feet are trying to take her in different directions," Bingley said.

"Yes, indeed," Darcy agreed. "A man will wish to be vigilant dancing with such a partner if he does not want to literally fall into the parson's mousetrap." A smile spread wide across his face.

"A trap you have successfully managed to evade for years, old man." Bingley clapped Darcy on the shoulder and laughed as Darcy gave him an exasperated look. "As I understand it, the marriage state is not to be feared."

"If you enter into it with the correct person, it is not, but I have seen enough unequal marriages to give me pause."

"Be that as it may, you will never find the right person if you continue to limit your socializing to those people with whom you are already acquainted." Bingley folded his arms across his chest and wore a conceited sort of grin. He had managed to manoeuvre the conversation very neatly back to where it had been and with a solid argument for why Darcy should not refuse an introduction.

"I believe," Bingley continued, "that I had offered to arrange for an introduction, and you were saying something about the lady being tolerable or some such drivel before we were interrupted. Please continue."

Darcy opened his mouth to continue with his cruel prevarication but abruptly closed it again as he realized that they now stood mere feet away from the lady, and since Bingley had spun him, the beguiling young woman was no longer behind him but was rather directly in front of him. There was no way Darcy could spout such ungentlemanly and untrue sentiments as he had planned within her hearing. How could he behold the beauty before him and call it anything but what it was? He caught her eye again and saw the displeasure that resided there.

Had she heard what he had said earlier or was it only what Bingley had repeated just now? It really did not matter which she had heard. Either way, he was the source of her displeasure. There was nothing for it but to confess to his dishonesty. He spoke to Bingley but looked at her. "Forgive me, I was not being truthful."

He saw her blink in astonishment. "You are right, as you often are about a lady's beauty. She is most decidedly lovely."

A faint blush crept up her cheeks. It was quite becoming.

He looked at Bingley. "I would like nothing better than to be introduced. Perhaps, I might even be persuaded to dance. In fact, if you promise to stop your entreaties, I will agree to one dance with someone I have just met if she will allow it."

Miss Bennet's sister was regarding her hands which were folded tightly in her lap, but she was unmistakably smiling. At least he need not fear rejection.

"Yes, yes," Bingley said. "I know you do not dance unless forced and then only with partners with whom you are particularly acquainted. You have a difficult enough time just speaking to someone new without having to remember your footing while doing so."

Apparently, Bingley had been listening to him, but must he spout such information now when Darcy hoped to make a favourable impression on the lady who could clearly hear what was being said? Darcy could feel his cheeks becoming warm.

"Have no fear my taciturn friend," Bingley continued, "Miss Bennet assures me that her sister has words enough for two people, so a conversation with her shall not tax you too overly much."

Darcy bit the insides of his cheeks to keep from laughing at the glare the young lady leveled at Bingley's back.

"Miss Bennet," Bingley called across three people as the lady approached her sister. "My friend wishes for an introduction to your sister."

No, Darcy thought with a groan, subtlety was not Bingley's forte. He winced as Miss Bennet's sister's cheeks grew crimson, which probably matched his own as they were feeling exceedingly warm.

Miss Bennet curtseyed to Darcy and, with a smile, introduced him to her sister Miss Elizabeth. Immediately after which, Bingley claimed Miss Bennet for the next dance and swiftly led her away, leaving Darcy and Miss Elizabeth quite alone in the sea of people that filled Meryton's assembly hall.

For a moment, Darcy stood silently in front of Miss Elizabeth not knowing what to say and mentally rebuking his friend. Could Bingley not even afford a moment to ease him into a conversation? Darcy fumbled a bit with some pleasantries before getting to the point.

"Do you dance, Miss Elizabeth?"

"I do when asked, Mr. Darcy." She quirked an eyebrow and waited.

"My apologies, that did not come out as I meant it to do." Darcy gave a small self-deprecating laugh. "I believe what I meant to ask was, do you wish to dance, Miss Elizabeth?"

The half-smile that she wore twitched. Darcy was sure that she was going to laugh, but she managed to suppress the urge. Her eyes, however, danced in merriment. It was a dance he could watch happily for hours.

"Indeed, I do wish to dance. Did you have a particular partner in mind for me?"

He could hear the laughter in her tone. She was provoking him purposefully. He shook his head, which strangely no longer pounded, and chuckled at his own foolishness. "I had rather hoped to be your partner for this set if that is acceptable to you?"

The small half-smile she wore spread into a full smile of genuine pleasure, encompassing not just her mouth but also her eyes. "I believe that would be tolerable, sir." She placed her hand on his proffered arm.

Did she think to continue to tease him? He had survived his fair share of uncomfortable moments this evening already. He could likely weather one more. He looked down at her and raised an eyebrow while a most unfamiliar expression – a smirk – curled his lips. "And I believe, Miss Elizabeth, that it would be lovely."

Chapter 2

A HORRIBLE SQUAWK FROM a violin pierced the air. Darcy cringed. The sound was not foreign to him. How many times had he made that same nerve-grating sound when learning to play?

"I suppose our musicians are not of the quality you are used to hearing," Miss Elizabeth said.

Her comment took him by surprise. Why was she apologizing for the error of another?

"It is the first error I have noticed tonight," he answered. "I think that is admirable, especially since one of the members of the ensemble looks rather young." The lad to whom he referred appeared to be no more than twelve. Darcy had been watching him on and off all evening and the boy was remarkably good for his age.

"I believe he is. This is his first assembly, but I have heard him play at a dinner party at Lucas Lodge."

"He is doing very well then."

Her brow furrowed. "Do you truly think so?"

Why did she doubt him? Did he appear to be the sort who lied? The thought prickled.

"I would not say it if I did not think it. I am not the sort of gentleman who tells falsehoods to impress a lady." Indeed, he abhorred deceit.

Momentary surprise widened her eyes before she regained her composure, though her eyes took on a cool edge as did her voice. "I did not mean to offend you, Mr. Darcy."

She took her place next to him for the dance and looked away from him and toward those who had formed their group with them. She even smiled at the gentleman across from her, but her smile faded the instant the music began and her eyes returned to him.

Darcy's own feelings of offense faded and were quickly replaced with guilt. Next to suspicion, guilt was likely the emotion with which Darcy was most familiar. They had always been unwelcome companions of his, but after discovering that the companion he had hired for his sister had played a role in Georgiana's near ruin this summer, the two had come to set up a grand house in his mind and seemed to always be lurking in the shadows.

"I did not mean to offend you, Miss Elizabeth," he offered as an apology when they joined hands to begin the patterns of the dance.

One of her eyebrows arched in disbelief. "You did say you were not being truthful when speaking to Mr. Bingley."

Her words hit him in the abdomen as firmly as any of his sparring partner's punches ever had. It was a good thing that this cotillion was one with which he was familiar since his feet needed to move him along without much help from his brain at that moment. Having one's faults so handily stated by a pretty young lady was both humbling and distracting. Would any lady, with whom he had ever danced before this, have challenged him so directly? He doubted it.

"You are correct," he said when they next joined hands. "Your questioning was not out of place. I apologize."

Her lips curved into a pleased expression, and again, Darcy was thankful that this dance was one he knew well.

"May I then conclude that you have enjoyed the music this evening?" she asked before they were once again parted.

Darcy wound his way through the steps which only allowed a brief touch of hands with Miss Elizabeth before he had to circle away once again. Finally, they were reunited by the pattern.

"I have indeed enjoyed the music this evening," he assured her.

"Are you a great lover of music?"

"I am. How about you, Miss Elizabeth? Do you enjoy music?"

"Very much, sir."

"I am happy to hear it."

"Have you enjoyed anything else about the evening?" Again, she asked the question just before the dance snatched her away from him.

It was several steps before they were rejoined, and the dance ended.

"This dance," he said as he bowed. "I have enjoyed this dance." He held out his hand to her.

"And is that it?" she asked as she placed her hand in his. "Is that all you have enjoyed this evening – one dance and some music?"

She was teasing him. He could hear it in her voice, and yet, he did not suspect her of doing so with any design other than to continue a conversation. The thought was excessively delightful.

"I have enjoyed our limited conversation," he admitted. "I hope we can continue it during the next dance."

"A dance would be very dull without any discussion," she assured him. "What shall our next topic of conversation be?"

"Have we concluded all there is to know about music?" he asked as the first notes of a reel signalled them to begin.

"I think we may have said so much as can be said during a dance."

The ever-interfering dance patterns once again came between them. Normally, Darcy was all for the music and dance steps limiting the amount of time he had to spend discussing any topic with a lady. But that was not the case with Miss Elizabeth. She did not bat her lashes or duck her head and feign being demure. She spoke to him as if she were genuinely interested in his thoughts and not just his fortune. He hoped he was not mistaken in that.

"And when shall we canvas what remains of the topic of music?" he asked while they waited for the couple next to them to pass down the line.

"I suppose that is up to you, sir."

Had she drawn him along to trick him into asking to call on her?

"Have I offended again?" she asked quietly when he said nothing.

His brow furrowed. "No, I do not believe you have."

"But you are uncertain?" Her tone was incredulous.

"I was thinking."

"Indeed?" That one eyebrow of hers was arching in disbelief again.

"Yes. I do think occasionally," he said dryly. "In fact, I do it quite often."

Her lips were pressed together as if attempting to contain a laugh when the music once again pulled them apart, and Darcy wanted nothing more than to take her by the hand and leave the dance floor so that they could talk without interruption. His frustration surprised him, and when he and Miss Elizabeth were once again given a chance to speak, he was unable to do so as he was attempting to not only decide whether or not he should call on her, but also to discover the source of his irritation.

"Are you still thinking?" Amusement danced in her eyes.

"Yes."

The dance required that they move, and he obliged. It was only a few steps to the end. Darcy was not certain he had ever been quite so happy to have a dance finished as he was at the conclusion of this particular dance. There had been dances which had been painful – the conclusion of which had brought immense relief for it meant he could return his partner to her guardian and be on his way. However, that was not why he was so thankful for the end of tonight's dance. Now that the dance was over, he could speak to Miss Elizabeth in unbroken thoughts.

"I am not certain when the best time is for us to conclude our discussion of music," he said as he led her from the dance floor. "We could walk and talk now, which is my preference, or I could call on you tomorrow."

"But?" she prompted when he fell silent.

He lowered his voice and attempted to make his tone warm and friendly. "I am uncertain which would be less likely to raise expectations."

"Ah."

Was that to be her only response? He glanced at her. Was she offended? He tried to read her expression. "I am not looking for a wife," he added.

"That is excellent news since I am not looking for a husband," she replied with a flutter of lashes.

"You are not?" Was not every young lady, who was a miss, looking for a husband?

"No, I am not."

Miss Elizabeth certainly was unusual. First, she was sitting with the wallflowers despite being enchantingly pretty. Then, she challenged him and did not simper and preen as other ladies seemed given to do. And now, she admitted she was not searching for a husband.

"It is not because I do not wish to marry," she said, just as he was wondering that very thing. "I just see no need to look for a husband as if I am stalking prey, nor do I wish to snare a gentleman or leg shackle him or see him in a parson's noose." She laughed lightly.

"You do not?" He had thought that all young ladies desired such things, for that is the way it had always appeared to him.

"Shall I shock you further?" she asked with laughing eyes.

"I do not think it is unusual that I should be surprised by such sentiments being shared with me," he said coolly.

"Mr. Darcy, I assure you that I have no desire to offend you."

He glanced to his left and then to his right before whispering. "Then, why are you laughing at me?"

Her eyes grew wide. "Laughing at you?"

"Yes." She was befuddling.

"I am not laughing at you. I am laughing at me and how horrified my mother would be to hear me speaking to you so openly."

"You are?"

She sighed. "I am. My mother would scold me most severely for my behaviour."

"Then, why do you..." He was not certain how to put his curiosity about her willfully unorthodox behaviour into words without causing offense.

"Love will find me."

His brow furrowed. How was that an answer to anything?

"I shall not marry without love, respect, and understanding. Not for all the money in the world. Therefore, I will not pretend to be what I am not."

"But to be so forward might be..." He grimaced and shook his head. He could not finish that thought without sounding disparaging.

"Yes, you are correct. It is a dangerous game, and I do not behave as I am doing at present with every gentleman who asks me to dance."

Darcy was not certain if that should be a relief or a source of further concern.

"You seem to think that since you deigned to ask me to dance that I would set my cap at you," she said as if his thoughts were clearly written on his face and begging to be answered.

"I thought nothing of the sort," he retorted.

Her eyebrow arched in disbelief, scolding him without words. She was dangerous to his equilibrium. He had felt at sixes and sevens ever since he had attempted to refuse an introduction to her.

"Very well, I may have thought that, but it is only because that is how it always is." His ears burned with heat at the admission.

"I thought as much."

"You did?" A portion of his mind warned him to find an escape while another portion demanded that he discover more about the peculiar lady whose hand rested gently on his arm.

She laughed. "I am certain you heard the whispers about who you were and what fortune you have when you entered the room."

He had. It, too, was how it always was.

"When you brought up the fact that you are not looking for a wife, I wished to set your mind at ease. My cap is safely stored at home and not available to be set at anyone. Not even the master of Pemberley who owns half of Derbyshire and is said to have ten thousand a year."

He smiled in response to her smile.

"Not even," she continued as a faint blush stained her cheeks, "if dancing with him was lovely just as he said it would be."

She thought dancing with him was lovely? The thought was endearing while being at the same time suspiciously flirtatious. However, he believed her when she said she was not trying to snare him.

"Not even then?" Darcy managed to force out of his conflicted mind.

"Not even then."

"Why?"

"Because love will find me, Mr. Darcy."

Ah, so he only had a chance of marrying her if he loved her.

"I see."

Marry her? Since when did his mind jump so quickly from a lovely dance and an interesting conversation to marriage?

She laughed. "I fear you are still confused."

He shrugged. "Let us just agree that you have given me something to ponder later."

They had wandered down the full length of the ballroom and were now standing near the doors that led out to a small garden with a well-lit path. For a moment, Darcy considered asking her to walk with him there.

"Ah, Darcy, there you are! And I see you still have your dance partner with you."

"We were just going to discuss music," Darcy said to Bingley.

Bingley smirked. "Were you indeed?"

"Yes," Miss Elizabeth answered. "However, if you are in need of Mr. Darcy's attention, I shall go find my sister, and our discussion of music can be postponed until another time." She removed her hand from Darcy's arm. "Thank you, sir, for the dance." She dipped a curtsey.

"It was my pleasure," he said with a bow. "May we continue our discussion tomorrow?" he added.

"That would be perfect."

"Until then," he said before she scooted away, and he watched her go instead of following after her as he for some inexplicable reason wished to do.

"Was it truly your pleasure?" Bingley wore a self-satisfied grin.

Darcy was still watching Miss Elizabeth wind her way through the crowd, stopping now and again to say something to the people she passed. Meeting and dancing with her had most certainly been a pleasure, but did he wish to admit such a thing to his friend? Not at present.

"It was tolerable," he said with a silent chuckle as he stepped out into the garden with his bothersome friend, who was not willing to believe Darcy's answer, at his heels.

Chapter 3

A WELL-WORN PATH, WINDING its way through the Hertfordshire countryside, lay in front of Darcy, and a pretty lady walked at his side. This was not how Darcy had imagined his call at Longbourn to go. He had expected to spend fifteen minutes to half an hour in the sitting room feeling very ill-at-ease and struggling to engage in polite conversation, which he hoped he might be able to turn toward things which were not merely common topics of conversation so that he could learn more about Miss Elizabeth.

Instead, he had found himself standing in the sitting room at Longbourn for only five minutes while Bingley arranged to go for a walk with Miss Bennet with Darcy and Miss Elizabeth as proposed chaperones. Mrs. Bennet was so far beyond delighted to have Bingley showing such interest in her eldest daughter that neither Darcy nor Miss Elizabeth was given an opening to refuse being included in the walking party.

And that had brought Darcy to this wonderful prospect of fresh air, good exercise, and Miss Elizabeth's companionship.

"It is a beautiful day," he said, indulging, for the sake of comfort, in the commonest of conversation starters.

"Indeed, it is!" Bingley enthused from where he and Miss Bennet walked in front of Darcy and Miss Elizabeth.

"Take care." Bingley held out his hand to Miss Bennet as they came to a dip in the path which had not yet dried out after the rain of two days ago.

Darcy followed suit, extending his hand to Miss Elizabeth.

"I am very grateful to you for the suggestion of a walk," Miss Elizabeth called out to Bingley as she placed her hand in Darcy's and neatly stepped over the offensive patch of mud. "I am not fond of sitting inside on fine days," she added just for Darcy's ears.

"Think nothing of it," Bingley replied. "Darcy does not do well in parlours, and there is a greater chance of being allowed to hold a pretty lady's hand on a walk than there is when sitting in a parlour." He tucked Miss Bennet's hand into the crook of his elbow.

Miss Bennet's head dipped, and Darcy imagined she likely smiled and blushed. However, he could not be certain for her bonnet blocked his view of her features somewhat.

"I prefer to walk unaided." Miss Elizabeth gave her hand a little tug to dislodge it from his.

"My apologies." He clasped his hands behind his back once again. It seemed to him that he did not do much better in the fresh air than he did in a sitting room. However, their walk had just begun, so he must not give up hope just yet.

They walked slowly behind Bingley and Miss Bennet. Darcy wished to have some distance between himself and his friend so that whatever he and Miss Elizabeth discussed would not be heard by Bingley, for he was not yet ready to share with his friend just how eager he was to know more about Miss Elizabeth. Added to that reason was the fact that Darcy figured Bingley would appreciate the privacy.

"Do you walk here often?" Darcy cast a glance at his walking partner.

"So often as I am able," she replied. "I adore a ramble through the countryside where there is no specific purpose other than pleasure."

"We are of one mind on that."

"Indeed?"

Did he hear delight in her tone? Perhaps this was a topic on which they could begin a discussion that was more intimate than the fickleness of the weather in England. For some reason, the source of which Darcy was not willing to consider, he found himself longing for some sort of intimate conversation with Miss Elizabeth, the sort of conversation which would deepen the bonds of friendship that had taken tentative root between them at the assembly.

"I find the lack of space to lose myself in my thoughts while enjoying nature to be one of the most restrictive aspects of town," he said, grasping onto what he hoped would be the beginning of satisfying his longing. "When I am home at Pemberley, there is ample space for such enjoyment. However, I do not always have so much time as I would like for the activity."

Stewarding an estate the size of Pemberley so that he could leave it in good condition with the sufficient income to sustain both itself and its inhabitants was a heavy weight to bear. He just hoped he was up to the challenge. His shoulders sagged for a moment on a sigh. He had thought himself more than adequate to take on the role of master of Pemberley – until recently.

"I would imagine that your knowledge will be helpful to Mr. Bingley," Miss Elizabeth said.

"I hope it will be," he answered honestly. With her, he felt no need to don some veil of what was expected rather than revealing who he was. It was a novel and wonderful feeling that stirred a sense of serenity within him.

They walked on a pace without speaking while Darcy surveyed the countryside and considered what he would recommend to Bingley as far as adding fields to his estate. Bingley had only let the manor house at Netherfield, but come spring or even before, should Bingley decide to take Netherfield on a more permanent basis, he would need to be prepared to petition for lands to be added. His inheritance, substantial as it was, would only take him so far. He must discover how to add to his holding and increase his income. He would, of course, look to Darcy for guidance in all of that. While Bingley was confident in many things, he was also excessively willing to take advice from those whom he trusted and viewed as experts.

"I am certain should not ask," Miss Elizabeth said, interrupting Darcy's thoughts about his friend's reliance on him. "And I do not mean to offend, but you seem to be very unsure of yourself." She smiled at him, probably to soften the blow of her words. "It is in stark contrast to how you carry your person."

"It is perplexing, is it not?" And he wished he could banish his feeling of inadequacy, but, thanks to what had happened at Ramsgate with his sister, he could not.

"Excessively," she agreed.

"I assure you that there is a reason for the disparity. However, it is not something of which I wish to speak." The idea of telling her crept into his mind but was quickly pushed aside. It was the first time he had considered talking about the incident with someone other than the few – his cousin, his uncle, and Bingley – who knew about it.

She watched him as they walked five more steps. Then, she turned away, causing a small flutter of trepidation to pass through him.

"To anyone," he added quickly. "I did not mean that I did not wish to speak of it only to you."

"I am not offended, Mr. Darcy. We all have our secrets."

That was true. However, he was certain any secret she might be concealing was nothing compared to the one he hid.

"For instance," she continued with a teasing glance in his direction, "I cannot play the piano without my fingers stumbling at least once during a performance."

His brow furrowed. "I am uncertain how that is a secret."

"Did you already know that? Has someone told you?"

If he did not know better, he would think she was flirting with him. But she was not. She was not looking to snare a husband. This was just how Miss Elizabeth was. It was a delightful thing for Darcy to be spoken to by a pretty young lady as she would speak to any acquaintance.

"No," he answered, "why should anyone tell me about your ability or lack of ability to play the piano?"

"You have a fortune, Mr. Darcy, and you are not married." She looked at him expectantly but when he said nothing, she continued. "Not everyone is so friendly as they appear. In fact, some very sweet looking ladies can be the shrewdest schemers."

Understanding dawned on him. "You mean someone would tell me such a thing to sway me away from considering you as a wife."

"Yes."

"It would be their folly," he said. "I am not looking for a concert pianist."

"That is good to know." Her enjoyment of their discussion shone in her expression. "Let me see." She paused, her brow furrowed, and her lips pursed as if thinking. "Oh, I know! I speak very few languages and only English with any great skill."

He chuckled at her willingness to share with him what she assumed to be her shortcomings.

"I am also not looking for a tutor, nor am I expecting my wife to be an emissary to the continent or beyond."

"You are not easily put off, Mr. Darcy," she said with a laugh. "I am well-read and opinionated." She walked slightly at an angle so that she could look at him.

"Ah, now, those are admirable qualities."

She laughed again. "You would wish for an opinionated wife? I simply cannot believe it."

Her merriment was infectious, and he felt his spirit buoyed up by it. "I hope that whomever I eventually marry, when I am ready to marry, has an opinion of her own rather than just parroting mine. However, I would also hope that she would be the sort of lady who did not flaunt her opinion publicly to my harm."

Her expression grew serious. "I hope I am never such a lady."

"But you are uncertain that you could always refrain from being such a wife?"

She grimaced and nodded. "I have a temper." She whispered the confession as if it was her most shameful secret.

"As do I," he assured her.

"Does your temper cause you to speak without thought and in the most hurtful way possible? For mine does." She averted her eyes from him and turned to walk facing forward instead of facing him.

"I have been known to speak cruelly when angry."

She turned her head to look at him. Her mouth hung slightly agape, and her eyes were wide.

"Have I surprised you?"

"You have."

"Why?"

She stopped walking and so did he. "I suppose I thought you would become cold, distant, and silent." Her lips tipped up on one side. "It seemed to fit how you carry yourself."

The way he stood and walked made him appear as if he would be cold? "Do you mean to tell me that I appear to be arrogant?"

Her grimace was reply enough.

"I am the master of a grand estate," he said cooly. "Pemberley is far larger than either Netherfield or Longbourn. I must look the part." By that he meant capable – whether he felt as if he was or not.

She studied his features and then held his gaze. "I should think," she said softly, "that the master of any estate would do better if he appeared to be both sure of himself and approachable."

He bristled at her words. Who was she to instruct him on such a subject?

"I apologize," she said when he turned from her and began walking again without speaking. "I have angered you."

He looked in her direction and arched an eyebrow in question. She pressed her lips together as if she were attempting not to laugh.

"You became silent," she whispered. "I did not mean to offend you." Her brow furrowed. "We seem to say that a great deal."

She was right. They had spent a great deal of time in their short acquaintance either being offended or apologizing for causing offense.

"We do," he admitted. However, it was better that they apologized rather than carrying on as if the offense had never happened. Letting a misunderstanding or careless words fester was never a good thing. Being quick to ask for forgiveness was an admirable quality to list to his reasons for admiring Miss Elizabeth.

"I play the violin," he said to break the silence which had crept in between them. "Often without any painful squeaks."

"That is admirable."

"I speak French and can read Latin."

"Impressive."

"Not overly," he assured her. "My cousin can speak French and Spanish and understands enough German that he would be able to survive in a Germanic land if needed, which is beneficial to him since has spent time on the continent as part of His Majesty's forces."

"Ah, a soldier."

Darcy nodded. "A colonel."

"Are you close to him?"

Again, Darcy nodded. He and Richard were more like brothers than cousins. "We share guardianship of my sister."

"You have a sister?"

"I do. She is several years younger than I."

"You will have to tell me about her someday."

"Someday?" he asked in surprise. "Not today?" Why did she not wish to speak about his sister?

"Oh, you can tell me about her today if you wish, but do you remember the stream Jane mentioned when we were deciding to where we should walk?"

"I do."

"We are nearly there."

And they were. The time it took from them to walk from where they were to where the stream was would not have been enough time to tell her all there was to tell about his sister.

Bingley and Miss Bennet were already seated on a large rock near the water's edge when Darcy and Elizabeth joined them.

"We thought we were going to have to send out a search party for you," Bingley teased. "You are not usually such a slow walker, Darcy."

"His legs are much longer than Elizabeth's. I am certain Mr. Darcy was only being gentlemanly," Miss Bennet replied.

"I am certain you are correct," Bingley assured her, which earned him a demure smile instead of some teasing quip such as "I am, am I not?"

It was too agreeable an exchange. Far too agreeable. There was no spark of excitement in being so like-minded. While that sort of arrangement was what some sought, and there was nothing wrong with it per se, it was not what Darcy preferred. As much as he always said he longed for peace in his life, he did not wish for it so much that he wanted all disagreements to cease. He could not think of one friend in his inner circle who did not aggravate him to some extent. Whomever he married would likely also provoke him at times. His gaze fell on Miss Elizabeth. Would she not be surprised to hear that?

"Is Miss Bennet right?" Bingley pressed when Darcy did not reply.

"About what?" He turned to see his friend smirking at him.

"About you walking slowly because of your companion's legs being shorter than yours."

He shook his head. "No, that is not why we were walking slowly."

"It is not?" Bingley actually looked surprised. How delightful!

"We were admiring the countryside and talking. A wander through nature is a great way to order one's thinking. The land looks as if it produces well."

"Oh, yes," Miss Bennet agreed, "I believe it does. Papa does not complain about the fields very often, does he, Lizzy?"

"No, never." There was a sardonic note to her tone. "Only when it does not rain or when it is too rainy or when the spring is too cold or the summer too warm." She fluttered her lashes at her sister.

Miss Elizabeth was certainly not too agreeable. She possessed spirit and from the way her sister huffed, she was good at drawing a bit of spirit out of others.

"That is normal," Miss Bennet retorted.

"If Darcy says it looks productive, I believe him," Bingley inserted.

"Without verifying his supposition?" Miss Elizabeth asked in surprise.

Bingley blinked. "Darcy's knowledge about producing crops and tending livestock is excellent."

"I will not argue with you on that. I am only saying that a cursory glance at a field or two might not be evidence enough."

"She is right," Darcy said before Bingley could do more than open his mouth to reply. "While I think my opinion is correct, it would be good to have it supported by anecdotes from your neighbours."

"Perhaps when we go shooting with Sir William?" Bingley cast a glance in Miss Elizabeth's direction as if to gain her approval of the idea.

"What do you think, Mr. Darcy?" Miss Elizabeth asked him.

"Would Sir William be knowledgeable?" he asked her.

Her lips tipped into a smile.

Was there a prettier sight than her smiling at him as she was now? He was certain it would take years of searching to find it if, indeed, such a sight could be found.

"If there is anything to know in Hertfordshire, Sir William knows it, and," her brows flicked up quickly as if to say the next part of what she had to say was significant, "he rarely goes shooting without my father joining him."

"Ah." Her father was the key then. He would be certain to ask Mr. Bennet about the productivity of the fields in the area.

"Then, it is an excellent idea, Bingley." His eyes did not leave Miss Elizabeth's. "Shall we follow the stream for a distance?"

"I had hoped to sit for a while," Miss Bennet said softly.

"Then, sit," Miss Elizabeth said to her sister, pulling her gaze away from his, seemingly, with some effort. "I am nearly certain I can keep Mr. Darcy from getting lost."

"And I shall make certain nothing dreadful befalls your sister," Darcy added.

Bingley was smirking again, but Darcy did not care. Let him smirk and gloat. Having Miss Elizabeth's company all to himself was worth a bit of bother.

"Shall we?" He held out his hand to her.

She said not a word in reply but silently placed her hand in his proffered one.

Chapter 4

"I MUST THANK YOU for mentioning my need to discover what I can about the area, and Netherfield in particular, to your father," Darcy said two weeks later as, once again, he and Miss Elizabeth played chaperone to Bingley and Miss Bennet.

The four of them taking a walk had become a bit of a ritual when it was not raining. He and Bingley would arrive at Longbourn and spend five or ten minutes in the sitting room before Mrs. Bennet would dismiss them to take a walk. The lady was openly eager to promote the match between Miss Bennet and Bingley, but she appeared to be blind to the attachment forming between Darcy and Miss Elizabeth.

However, from what Mr. Bennet had said while he was out shooting with Darcy and Bingley, Darcy was positive that Mrs. Bennet was more cunning than one might suppose when it came to promoting a match to her second eldest daughter. According to her husband, she had told him about Darcy's attentions toward Miss Elizabeth, and then, after quite skillfully shooting three birds, Mr. Bennet had pointed out that he was still a good shot. The comment had been accompanied by a pointed look and a confession from Darcy that his intentions were honorable.

"Between what I have learned from him and what Sir William has shared with me, I am doubly certain that Netherfield would be an excellent choice of an estate for my friend should he find it to his liking."

Darcy undoubtedly knew far more about the news of Meryton than most, thanks to Sir William. That gentleman was most assuredly an excellent resource for interesting tales. While he was entertaining and his stories did provide insight about the community into which Bingley was proposing to plant himself, Darcy had been thankful to have Mr. Bennet with them on that hunting excursion. For, it was Mr. Bennet who had been the source of the most useful information. He had shared all he knew about the fields surrounding Netherfield and who was leasing which bit and what was being raised on that ground. The gentleman's mind was as keen as his shooting.

"Do you think Mr. Bingley will take Netherfield?" Miss Elizabeth asked.

Darcy shrugged. "I am not certain. He seems to like the place well enough, but should he choose to settle on Netherfield, it will mean bearing with an abundance of grumbling from his sisters – Miss Bingley, in particular, though Mrs. Hurst will support her." Mrs. Hurst always supported Miss Bingley in an argument. Darcy did not envy Bingley's task of trying to keep either of his sisters somewhat mollified. The two ladies were a testy pair, each of whom liked to have her own way.

"Do Mr. Bingley's sisters not like Netherfield?"

Miss Elizabeth removed her hand from Darcy's arm and placed her hand in his when he offered it, for they had come to that dip in the path which had, on their first walk along this trail, been muddy. It was dry now, and there was no need for her to require assistance over the depression. However, that did not keep Darcy from offering it, and then tucking her hand into the crook of his arm once again and holding it there. She had never pulled her hand away from him since that first walk. In fact, she always seemed delighted when he offered his arm to her.

"They do not like Hertfordshire," Darcy answered.

"Not like Hertfordshire? I cannot see how that can be."

"Neither can I." Though to be honest, he had at one time been just as determined as Miss Bingley and Mrs. Hurst were to dislike the place. That was, however, before he had discovered just how enchanting one particular lady, who called the county her home, could be.

"I suppose," that enchanting lady said, "that Meryton is nothing compared to London."

"Are you attempting to find reasons to excuse Miss Bingley's and Mrs. Hurst's unwarranted criticism?" he asked in an affected somber tone to tease her.

"No," she replied quickly. Her small smile let him know that she heard the taunt in his voice. "I am only attempting to reconcile such faulty thinking with the intelligence that Miss Bingley and her sister seemed to portray when I first met them."

He chuckled. "If I were to surmise a reason, I would lay the fault for their poor opinion at my feet."

"Indeed? Please, do tell, sir. I am all curiosity."

"You would have to see Pemberley to understand completely because Pemberley is the ambition of Miss Bingley."

"Has she set her cap at you?"

Darcy nodded. "She has no hope of ever gaining Pemberley. However, that is the standard to which she will compare any house her brother considers, and Netherfield pales in comparison to Pemberley House. I do not say that arrogantly. It is the truth."

Miss Elizabeth turned her head so that she could examine him. "You have piqued my curiosity further, sir. Does your staff give tours of the house?"

"Yes. Why?" He hoped it was because she wished to see it.

"My aunt and uncle Gardiner are known to travel to Derbyshire on occasion, and they have spoken about taking me with them on one of their journeys."

"And would you ask them to tour Pemberley if you joined them on their trip?"

She nodded. "If it is not too far from Lambton, I would. That is where my aunt grew up and where she returns to visit her family. Do you know it?"

"Lambton?" He knew Lambton very well.

"Yes."

"It is the closest market town to Pemberley."

"How perfect!" she cried.

Indeed, it was. A visit to Pemberley from Lambton would be very convenient, as would be a visit to Lambton from Pemberley. Of course, if he were successful in changing her mind about not looking for a husband, as he had just last night decided to do, her aunt and uncle could stay with them at Pemberley.

"Where does your aunt live now?"

"She and my uncle make their home in Gracechurch Street in London."

"Your uncle is in trade, then?"

Miss Elizabeth nodded. "And he is very successful, according to what I hear my mother say that my father does not correct." She looked at him apologetically. "Sometimes my mother does not remember details so well as she thinks she does, but that is not to say she is not clever."

Darcy had no doubt that Mrs. Bennet was clever in her own way – especially when it came to promoting her daughters. "We all excel at different things," he assured her.

"Indeed, we do," she agreed. "If you have not already surmised it, my mother's area of expertise involves all things social and domestic. She hosts the best dinner parties, and we are never in want of variety for meals. Nor do my sisters and I lack training in managing a home and sewing and stitching."

That was good to know. Both for himself and his friend. Bingley needed a lady who was well-versed in such things to stand by his side at Netherfield. Despite Miss Bennet's excessively agreeable demeanor, Darcy was beginning to understand why Bingley favoured her. Her serenity seemed to balance Bingley's exuberance perfectly.

"Does your sister admire my friend?"

"Can you not tell?" Miss Elizabeth asked in surprise.

"No," Darcy admitted. "I believe she must, but there seems to be no more pleasure in her seeing him than there is in her meeting with anyone else. Perhaps she is just too guarded." He knew that feeling intimately. He was always attempting to guard himself against appearing to be too enamoured with anything or anyone. There was the master of Pemberley image to keep intact, after all.

Miss Elizabeth was studying him again when he glanced in her direction. "So long as you do not tell her I said so, I can assure you that she is more than a little smitten with your friend. Are the feelings mutual?" She looked away. "I would hate for Jane to have her heartbroken."

Instinctively, Darcy's free hand covered Miss Elizabeth's hand which lay on his arm, and his thoughts turned to his own sister for a moment before he replied. Thankfully, Bingley was not the sort to toy with the heart of a lady. "I believe her affection is returned in equal, if not greater, measure."

"Elizabeth!"

Both Darcy and Elizabeth turned toward where Jane stood just in front of the trees that grew along the banks of the stream.

"Come quickly." There was no mistaking the urgency in Miss Bennet's voice.

Miss Elizabeth removed her hand from Darcy's arm and lifting her skirts began running. Darcy followed suit.

"It is Tommy," Miss Bennet explained to Elizabeth. "He was playing while his brother was fishing and fell from a tree. He will not let Mr. Bingley touch him, but I know he will allow you."

"Tommy is one of the tenant's children." Elizabeth spoke in hushed tones to Darcy as they followed Jane. "We have always had a special friendship because..." She paused as if she did not wish to say why, but then she added, "because we both love cats."

Perhaps later, she would tell him the true connections she had to the injured lad, who looked to be about eight years old and was lying on the ground under a tree. Another boy who must be his brother and only a year or two older sat beside him, rubbing Tommy's left arm.

"Miss Lizzy is here," the brother said.

"How long ago did this happen?" Darcy whispered to Miss Bennet as he began to remove his coat.

"Robert says a quarter-hour."

"Tommy is awake?"

"Yes." Miss Bennet looked to be on the verge of tears. Hers was a tender heart. "I am not so good with injuries as Lizzy is." Her tone was apologetic.

"We will do our best for him," Darcy assured her.

Leaving her, he went to where Elizabeth knelt beside Tommy. "Wrap him in this." He handed his jacket to Elizabeth.

"Tommy," Elizabeth spoke calmly and softly to the child, "what hurts?" As she tucked Darcy's coat around the boy's chest and arms, he winced. "Your arm?"

"Yes."

Young Tommy was doing his best not to cry, although from the looks of his face, he had shed a few tears before they arrived to help him.

"And my head," he added.

"Not your legs or back?" Darcy asked.

"This is my friend, Mr. Darcy," Elizabeth said to the boys, "and the other gentleman is my friend, Mr. Bingley. Do your legs or back hurt, Tommy?"

"No."

That was a relief. A broken arm and a bump to the head, which had not rendered the child unconscious, were not so dire as broken legs or injured backs. The former were not without their dangers, of course, but the latter could cripple a person.

"Your knife, Bingley," Darcy said as he untucked his shirt. "Is it the top of your arm or the bottom that hurts?"

"The bottom." Tommy looked at him warily.

"Miss Bennet, could you find two straight sticks the length of Tommy's forearm, please? Sturdy ones." Darcy took the knife Bingley handed him and began to cut a strip of material off his shirttails.

"What are you doing?" Miss Elizabeth asked.

"We must stabilize the injured arm before we move him. This is for tying the sticks to the arm." He pulled on the fabric to quicken the process of making bandages. "Check his head for blood."

"I knew to do that." The look she gave him was not a pleased one.

"My apologies. I am only thinking of Master Tommy." That earned him a quick smile before she turned back to the lad.

"It is not bleeding. I looked," Robert said. "Ran my hand behind his head and everything."

"Good man," Darcy said with a smile for the boy. "You are lucky to have such a smart brother, Master Tommy. Did you catch any fish?" Distraction often lessened the pain of a wound. His cousin, Richard, had taught him that.

"Two," Tommy answered. "But I did not catch them, Rob did."

"Are they big enough for dinner?"

"Yes, sir."

"And they will make a fine broth, too, I would imagine."

"Yes, sir."

Darcy nodded for Miss Bennet to give the sticks she had found to her sister. "Miss Elizabeth is going to need to move your arm a little while we tie the bandage on."

The child's eyes grew wide with fear.

"I will not lie to you, Master Tommy. It will not feel good. I know. My cousin had to do the same for me when I was about your age. Trees are notoriously tricky to climb." He looked at Bingley. "Your hand, please." He turned back to Tommy. "You can squeeze my friend's hand as hard as you want. Focus on that. And, crying is expected, or I shall feel very foolish for I cried when my cousin splinted my arm."

Tommy gave him a small wavering smile and a nod of understanding before squeezing his eyes closed.

"Are you ready, Miss Elizabeth?"

Her eyes held his while she nodded. There was some sort of softness about her expression that he could not quite define.

"I will hold your feet, Tommy. Are you ready?"

The child's chest rose and fell twice before he nodded.

Miss Elizabeth was very quick in setting the child's lower arm and hand between the sticks and tying them in place. The final strip of Darcy's shirt was used to create a sling to keep the arm lying across the boy's chest. That was the part which had brought the most tears.

"How far is it to your home?"

"It is a half-mile from Longbourn," Elizabeth answered.

Half a mile was a good distance to walk while carrying a child. Darcy rubbed his neck as he thought. The lad could not be allowed to walk in his injured state. Carrying him was the only option. It had to be done if the boy would trust him.

"Miss Bennet and I will go ahead and see if a cart can be made ready," Bingley offered.

Darcy shook his head. "My carriage would not need to be made ready. Tell my coachman that his services are needed to see Masters Robert and Tommy home. And, I am sure this could go without saying, but I shall say it anyway. See that someone goes for the surgeon."

Bingley gave a sharp nod of his head and, offering his hand to Miss Bennet, hurried with her toward Long-bourn.

"I am going to carry you, Tommy. I will do my best to keep you comfortable, but it will not be without pain."

"However," Miss Elizabeth inserted, "it must be done. We cannot leave you here. Will you let Mr. Darcy carry you? Both Robert and I will be right beside you." She dried the child's tears and brushed at one of her own.

"I will," Tommy said.

The way that the child looked at Miss Elizabeth said he would do whatever she asked him to do. She would be a wonderful mother. The thought only added to Darcy's determination to persuade Miss Elizabeth to marry him.

Carefully, Darcy scooped Tommy up. He was far lighter than Darcy had expected him to be, and Darcy hoped that the fish which had been caught were of substantial size.

"Get your basket and poles," Darcy said to Robert, who scampered away to fetch their fishing gear.

An hour and a half later, Darcy breathed a sigh of relief as he exited the cottage that Tommy and Robert called home. Tommy was in bed, and the surgeon had set the broken arm correctly. All that was left for Darcy to do, since he had sent his carriage back when they arrived, was to walk to Longbourn with Miss Elizabeth.

Miss Elizabeth wrapped her arm around his. "Thank you."

"For what? For that?" He looked back at the cottage.

"Yes. Tommy is not only special because he likes cats."

"I suspected as much."

"There was no time to explain it then," she said. "And it is true that both he and I like cats."

"Will you tell me now?" He drew her a little closer to his side.

"Of course," she replied with a smile. "Tommy is so special to me because I was there when he was born. Mama and I were calling on the tenants. Mrs. Evans was not supposed to have her baby for another three weeks, but Tommy was impatient. He was so tiny that the midwife was certain he would not survive." Her voice faltered on the word survive, and she paused for a moment before continuing. "Mama was not pleased, but Papa allowed me to spend several hours a day in that cottage, helping Mrs. Evans until we knew that Tommy had a better chance of living. Usually, my help consisted of holding Tommy. He was so tiny," she repeated. "I would sing to him and Robert and read them stories so their mother could rest."

"He is a very strong little fellow." He had to be to survive when he was not supposed to. "Will you visit him every day until he is healed?"

She shook her head. "Not every day."

"You will make sure he has enough to eat, will you not?"

She nodded. "I know his parents feed him so well as they are able, and they are not destitute. However…"

"He will not be able to help provide anything for them."

Again, she nodded.

"Do you think his parents would allow his brother to go fishing with Bingley and me?"

Her replying smile was beautiful. "I think they would allow you to do whatever you wished, sir."

"I did what had to be done."

"While that may be true, you did it in such a gentle way, but do not worry, sir, the secret that you have a good and tender heart is safe with me."

He smiled at her comment.

"You have a beautiful smile." Her eyes grew wide, and she pressed her lips together as if she should not have said what she did.

"You think so?"

She nodded.

"Do you think it helps me look more approachable?"

"You are not still thinking about what I said on that walk, are you?"

Darcy took a deep breath and released it slowly. This was his chance to discover if she would welcome his suit. "I have done very little except think about you and what you have said to me since our first dance." She had filled his thoughts during the day and his dreams at night.

She looked at him in surprise but said nothing.

He pressed on, hoping that her silence meant he had a chance of winning her and not that she hoped he would stop speaking. "I assure you I am still not looking for a wife."

Her brow furrowed. Was that sadness in her eyes?

His gaze held hers. "I believe I have found her, for you, Miss Elizabeth, have stolen my heart."

Her free hand flew to her heart. "Oh, my."

Encouraged by the fact that she appeared to be pleasantly surprised by his confession, he pressed on. "May I speak to your father?"

A smile spread rapidly across her face before she began to laugh. Had he misspoken?

She released his arm, pulled a small parcel of fabric, tied with a red ribbon, from her pocket, and handed it to him.

"What is this?" He turned it over in his hands.

"My cap."

"Your cap?" Had she come prepared to present it to him? He smiled. It seemed as if they were of one mind on how well they suited one another. That was a hopeful thought.

"If you remember, I said that I had tucked it away and had no plans to set my cap at anyone."

He nodded. He did remember that part of their conversation at the assembly. He remembered everything she had said.

"Do you remember why I had done so?" She pulled the corner of her bottom lip between her teeth and looked at him nervously.

Her words from the assembly replayed themselves in his mind.

"Has love found you?" Joy flooded him at the thought.

"I think he has." She shrugged one shoulder. "Or, at least, I hope he has."

"If I keep this," he lifted the parcel he held, "does it mean I have your permission to speak to your father?"

She nodded. "Yes, it and my heart are yours."

He looked to his left and then his right. It appeared as if they were alone. "May I kiss you?"

Her cheeks flushed but her eyes sparkled with mischief. "If anyone sees you, you will be stuck with me. Forever. Do you think you can tolerate that, sir?"

He stepped closer to her and, wrapping one arm around her, pulled her to him. "I think, Miss Elizabeth, that such a calamity would be absolutely delightful."

And with that, he lowered his lips to hers, sealing their agreement and claiming for himself the lady whom he knew would, despite his remaining uncertainty about his ability to rule his domain as it should be ruled, make his tolerable life into something which was truly, and magnificently, lovely.

If you enjoyed this book, be sure to let others know by leaving a review.

Want to know when other Leenie books will be available?
You can always know what's new with my books by joining one of my reader communities

leeniebrown.com/subscribe

More Books by Leenie

You can find all of Leenie's books at this link

bit.ly/LeenieBBooks

where you can explore the collections below

Dash of Darcy and Companions Collection

Marrying Elizabeth Series

Sweet Possibilities and Sweet Extras

Willow Hall Romances

The Choices Series

Darcy Family Holidays

Darcy and... An Austen-Inspired Collection

Teatime Tales (Sweet Austen-inspired Novelettes)

Other Pens

Touches of Austen

Nature's Fury and Delights (Sweet Regency Novelettes)

About Leenie

Leenie Brown has always been a girl with an active imagination, which, while growing up, was both an asset, providing many hours of fun as she played out stories, and a liability, when her older sister and aunt would tell her frightening tales. At one time, they had her convinced Dracula lived in the trunk at the end of the bed she slept in when visiting her grandparents!

Although it has been years since she cowered in her bed in her grandparents' basement, she still has an imagination which occasionally runs away with her, and she feeds it now as she did then — by reading!

Her heroes, when growing up, were authors, and the worlds they painted with words were (and still are) her favourite playgrounds! Now, as an adult, she spends much of her time in the Regency world, playing with the characters from her favourite Jane Austen novels and those of her own creation.

When she is not traipsing down a trail in an attempt to keep up with her imagination, Leenie resides in the beautiful province of Nova Scotia with her two sons and her very own Mr. Brown (a wonderful mix of all the best of Darcy, Bingley, and Edmund with a healthy dose of the teasing Mr. Tilney and just a dash of the scolding Mr. Knightley).

Connect with Leenie in one of her reader communities or on social media. Find links to all of those on her website at bit.ly/connect-with-leenie